Author
Erica London

Il
May

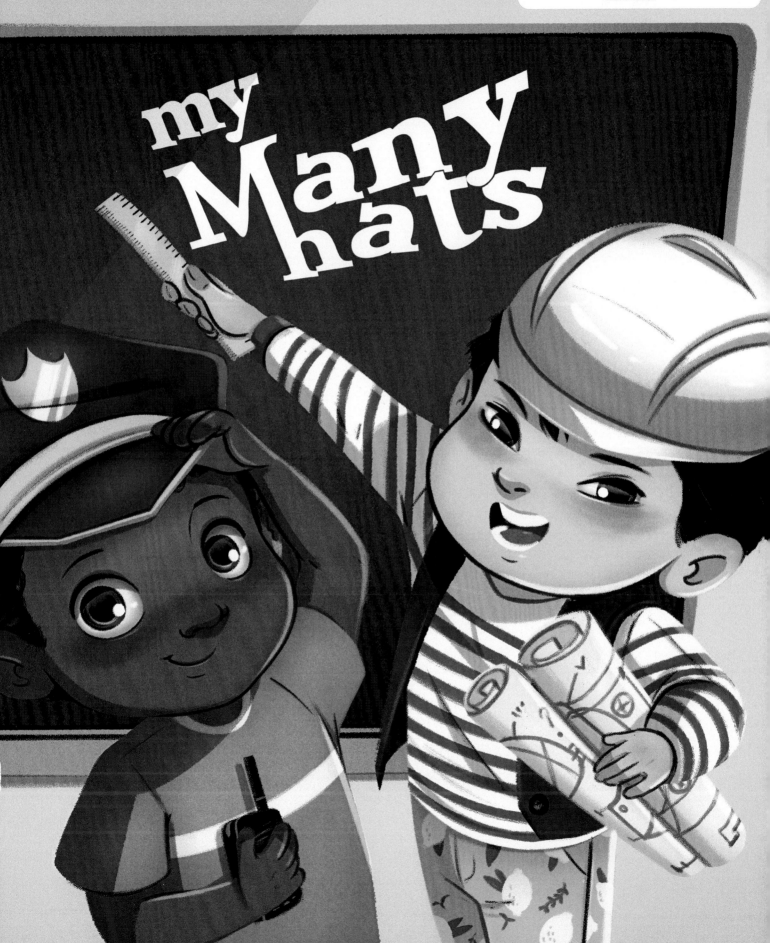

Dedication

"Everyone wears a different hat and deals with stuff differently, but we can do so much good in the world by standing together. We hope this book inspires you to not only search for your hat, but find out what hats your family members wear and recognize how hardworking they are!"

~ Mayhara and Erica

"Good morning, class. I hope you're all ready for your presentations today!" said Ms. Ansari cheerfully.

"I've been eager to see the creative ways you've found to present the many hats your parents wear."

"I believe we will begin with Steve and then Kiyoshi."

"First! Oh my goodness, it's a good thing I worked hard on this assignment. Okay Steve, breathe, you can do this! It's just a class... full of 15 students looking at you!" Steve thought to himself.

He walked to the front of the class, clutching his papers in his hand, hoping the words would come together just like he'd practiced at home.

He repeated the affirmation his parents taught him.

"I am smart, I am brave, I can do anything I put my mind to."
He was ready.

"Good morning. When Ms. Ansari told me about this assignment, I couldn't figure out what hats my parents could possibly wear. I mean, my dad is a police officer, so I suppose that could be a hat. My mother has never worked because she takes care of my sister and I, so I thought she didn't wear any hats."

"When I really stopped to think about it, I realized that my parents wear hats that I couldn't have imagined!"

"My dad is a hardworking officer who protects people in the community, and he is also an amazing chef. I think he can make stewed chicken and macaroni pie better than anyone."

"When we go boating on weekends, he makes sure we all have our life jackets on and we're safe. He even taught us how to perform CPR. He's OUR CAPTAIN!"

"My mother is the one we go to anytime we need help putting something together. Her father was a carpenter, so she knows EVERYTHING about woodworking."

"She put our beds together and she even renovated our kitchen on her own!" "Actually, we all chipped in and helped when we could. It was so much fun!"

"She takes the time to listen to all my problems and answers all the questions I have about almost anything. When I have math homework, she doesn't even need a calculator to help me. She's like my own personal guidance counselor and tutor."

"Upon completing this assignment, I realized that even though my parents didn't go to school for some of the things I mentioned, it has not stopped them from putting on those particular hats to provide for our family."

"Thanks for listening to my presentation," finished Steve. The whole class was silent. Steve wondered if it was because of something he said.

"I- I'm so sorry if I offended anyone," he stammered.

The class roared with cheers and praise. Students were shouting about how great his presentation was.

"Phew," breathed Steve as he wiped the sweat off his forehead.

"I did it, I actually did it!" he said to himself.

"Brilliant job, Steve. Kiyoshi, you're up next," said Ms. Ansari.

Kiyoshi was fine with presenting. He wasn't nervous at all. He skipped to the front of the class and bowed.

"Good morning Ms. Ansari, I know the assignment was to speak about the many hats our parents wear, but I thought it wouldn't make sense in my case because I'm the one who actually wears a lot of the hats," said Kiyoshi proudly.

"Oh my gosh, he's gonna fail, I'm sure of it. He didn't even follow the instructions," whispered Sophia to her friend.

Kiyoshi turned all shades of red, embarrassed by her comment.

Thankfully, the class ignored her, but Ms. Ansari was sure to handle it.

"Okay, Sophia, that is enough. Please continue, Kiyoshi," said Ms. Ansari as she waved him to proceed.

"Some of you know that my mother got into a car accident, and although she walked before, now she gets around in a wheelchair. I don't mind helping my mom because she has done so much for me."

All of a sudden, the proud look on Kiyoshi's face turned into one of reflection.

"On evenings after school, I wear the hat of a dishwasher. After my mom prepares dinner, it's my job to rinse the dishes and put them in the dishwasher."

"I also wear the hat of a gardener because I water the plants everyday before and after school."

"Our favourite thing to do, my mom and I, is work on projects together. I get to use a measuring tape and put on my construction hat. This is the reason why math is my favourite subject. My mom teaches me all the things she does at work, like calculating and measuring objects."

"You see, my mom is a mechanical engineer. She is very good at her job and although there are things she would like to do around the house that she obviously can't do anymore, we enjoy sharing hats. And you know what? She wears the best hat of all..."

"She's my MOM!" said Kiyoshi with pride.

Kiyoshi bowed once again to show the class he was not only finished, but also thankful for them taking the time to listen to his presentation.

Once again, the class exploded with chatter and a round of applause.

"I really love the way you made the assignment your own, Kiyoshi. So creative," smiled Ms. Ansari, nodding.

As Ms. Ansari made her way back to her desk, she had one question for a particular student.

"Sophia, what did you learn from the presentations today?" asked Ms. Ansari.

"That I can be anything I put my mind to... all I need is a hat," giggled Sophia. The class burst into laughter.

"Alright, I'll take that for an answer," smirked Ms. Ansari. "Well done, boys," she said to Steve and Kiyoshi.

"You see, students, one thing you should all remember is that you're capable and able to do so many things. Never limit yourself into thinking that you can only have one occupation, especially when we live in a world full of opportunities and possibilities. Truthfully, you don't need a hat to become anything; rather, you can make your own hat. And always remember to be respectful of others!"

 "I am a teacher, a mother, a painter, and a great scuba diver," said Ms. Ansari, making eye contact with each student.

"These are some of the many hats I wear!"

Ms. Ansari was interrupted by the bell.

Bringgggggg...

"Well, that's the bell! Have a wonderful evening. Let's repeat today's affirmation before you leave."

"If I can dream it, I can be it, because my gift will make room for me!" said the class all at once.

"Wonderful! Tomorrow we will continue with Heather and Vikram," said Ms. Ansari with a smile.

This book was solely inspired by Erica's parents, the people who wore and continue to wear hats she never thought possible. She's learnt through them that being a parent didn't mean she had to stop there. Why? Because we're capable of so much more.

We as INDIVIDUALS, as WOMEN are capable of so much more.

With all of Erica's books there comes a lesson to be learnt. In this one, it's to respect and appreciate the 'hats' your loved ones and friends wear because you never know. You might just end up wearing one of them some day.

Follow her on Instagram @colourtheirworld and visit her YouTube channel of the same name for more educational content.

We at Colour Their World are proud to have Mayhara Ferraz as our Principal Illustrator. Honestly, there's no distance that's too far for this Brazilian Native. Though she resides in Portugal, she is able to capture the mind of what Erica has envisioned for the characters in her Children's Books.

Having graduated with a degree in Visual Arts in Lisbon, she has perfected the art of drawing characters of colour of which is extremely important to Erica. "Collectively, we agree that having a true representation of children in literature is not only lovely to see, but essential. For this simple reason, it's why we will intentionally include children of all races in our books to come."